The Angel of Nitshill Road

Also by Anne Fine

How to Write Really Badly
The Country Pancake
Bill's New Frock
'The chicken gave it to me'
Anneli the Art Hater
Press Play
Scaredy Cat
Countdown
Design a Pram
A Sudden Puff of Glittering Smoke
A Sudden Swirl of Icy Wind
A Sudden Glow of Gold

Telling Tales – An Interview with Anne Fine

For older readers
The Summer House Loon
The Other Darker Ned
The Granny Project
The Stone Menagerie
Very Different

The Angel
of Nitshill Road
Anne Fine

Illustrated by Kate Aldous

EGMONT

First published in Great Britain 1992
by Methuen Children's Books Ltd
Reissued 2002 by Egmont Books Ltd
239 Kensington High Street
London W8 6SA

Text copyright © 1992 Anne Fine
Inside illustrations copyright © 1992 Kate Aldous
Cover illustration copyright © 2002 Lee Gibbons

The moral rights of the author and illustrators
have been asserted

ISBN 1 4052 0184 3

10 9 8 7 6 5 4 3

A CIP catalogue record for this title is
available from the British Library

Printed and bound by Cox & Wyman Ltd
Reading, Berkshire

Contents

'And the angel did wondrously . . .'
Judges, 13

1
Until the angel came . . .

Until the angel came, there were three terribly unhappy children at Nitshill Road School: Penny, Mark and Marigold. Shall we take Penny first?

Penny was plump. If you weren't friends with her, you might even say that she was getting on for fat. She had a pretty face, and lovely hair, and she was bright enough in class. But as the hands of the clock rolled round towards playtime she'd get a horrible feeling, as if her stomach was being gripped by a hard, invisible hand. However boring the lesson was, she wanted it to go on for ever and ever. Inside the classroom she was safe. Outside, Barry Hunter might go wheeling past, his arms stuck out like jet-plane wings, making the usual big show of having to swerve to avoid her.

'Beware of the mountain! Danger! Danger! The moving mountain is coming this way!'

'He's just stupid,' said Lisa, her friend. 'Ignore him.'

'You must treat him with the contempt he deserves,' said her father.

'Some people are just born pig-ignorant,' said her gran.

But Penny still felt terribly unhappy.

And so did Mark. Mark was small for his age. He had strange sticky-up hair, and he wore glasses thick as bottle-ends. He gnawed his fingernails and his pencils, and fussed and fidgeted, and even when he finally stopped racketing around the classroom and tried to sit down and work (not very well), he still got on everyone's nerves. But only Barry Hunter knew how to push him and push him and push him, till he flew into a temper.

'Mark the Martian!' he'd call from behind, imitating the rather peculiar stiff way Mark walked.

'Bionic eyes!' he'd shout, swooping up and peering through the thick lenses of Mark's spectacles.

'Controls not working properly?' he'd jeer, whenever Mark dropped a ball, or missed a kick, or ran into a wall by mistake.

And, sooner or later, unless the bell rang in time, Mark lost his temper – not like you or me, just getting red in the face and yelling, 'Oh, shut up, Barry Hunter! You're so stupid!' No. Mark went haywire, right out of control. With tears of rage spurting behind his glasses, he'd scream and howl and rush at Barry Hunter, trying to tear chunks of his hair out. Everyone turned to stare at him clawing and kicking and yelling. Some grinned quietly to themselves, but Barry Hunter laughed out loud. He was so big, he could hold Mark at arm's length and watch him flailing about like a windmill in a high gale. Then he'd tease him some more.

'Now, now, now! Temper, temper!'

Mark's elder sister said:

'Just stay right away from him, Mark. Then maybe he won't bother you.'

The teachers said:

'Really, Mark brings a lot of it on himself. He has to learn a bit of self-control. They'll have to sort themselves out.'

Mark's mother said:

'I'm going up to see the school if it doesn't stop.'

It didn't stop.

The third child was Marigold. Nobody knew that Marigold was unhappy. She never looked particularly sad, but then again, she never looked particularly happy. In fact, she never looked anything. A portrait painter

The Angel of Nitshill Road

would have had no trouble at all with Marigold. Her face never cracked into a smile, or darkened with a scowl. People had tried to make friends with her but they never got very far. She'd be away from school for a whole week, but only shrug when you asked what had been wrong with her. She'd hear your secrets, but she'd never tell you hers. In fact, come to think of it, she hardly ever spoke, even when Mr Fairway sighed over her slipshod and unfinished work, or Barry Hunter and his gang tormented her in the playground.

'Where do you live, Marigold? Is it that smelly street you walk down after school?'

Marigold didn't answer. Others did.

'Push off, Barry Hunter,' said some of the girls. 'Leave Marigold alone. Don't be so mean.'

'You don't exactly live in a palace yourself,' said the others.

But when the girls turned to smile at Marigold, she'd simply drift away, not even saying thanks. What was the point of sticking up for someone who doesn't care? You might as well leave her alone and get on with your own games.

'She can always join in if she wants,' they said to one another.

6

The Angel of Nitshill Road

'She doesn't mix at all,' the teachers said.

'I'd try and do something about it,' said the head teacher. 'But, honestly, she doesn't seem all that unhappy. I'm sure in this school we've got worse.'

But she was wrong. These were, by far, the most unhappy children in the school.

Until the angel came.

2
'Why are you all staring at me?'

Nobody thought she was an angel at first. Why should they? They were all milling about in the playground one morning before school began, when suddenly beside the high arched gates appeared a girl with a cloud of hair so gleaming bright that those who were standing near stared.

'Who's that?'

'I've never seen her before.'

'She must be new.'

And she did look new, in a way. Everything about her glowed like a freshly-minted coin.

The Angel of Nitshill Road

Her dress was so crisp it might have been ironed twice – inside and out. Her socks looked as if they had been pulled from the packet only a moment before. Her shoes were shop-shiny.

But she didn't look new in the other way. Most people look a bit nervous when they show up on their first morning at school, especially when it isn't even the first day of term, and they know everyone else will have had weeks and weeks, and maybe years, to find their way about and make good friends and learn the teachers' names. This newcomer didn't look in the slightest bit apprehensive. She was gazing around her as calm as you please. She looked at the stained brick walls, the peeling paint, the grimy windows and all the dustbins lined up along the wall. She read the rain-streaked sign over the door.

NITSHILL ROAD SCHOOL

Had she come all by herself?

By now, almost everyone in the playground

except for Marigold had turned to look at her.

She spread her hands and said in a ringing voice, clear as a bell:

'Why are you all staring at me? Am I fearfully late?'

Left to herself, Penny might have giggled. But Lisa poked her sharply in the ribs and, stepping forward, asked the girl with the shining cloud of hair:

'Have you come all by yourself?'

The newcomer gave a little shrug.

'My father was here, but he had to fly.'

Now it was Penny's turn to poke Lisa, to try and stop her giggling.

'What's your name?'

'Celeste.'

'*Celeste*?'

They didn't mean to be so rude. It just popped out.

The gold hair shimmered as Celeste tossed her head.

'It could have been worse,' she confided.

'Daddy was about to name me Angelica, but Granny swooped over just in time, and dashed the pen from his hand.'

Now people were gathering from all over the playground and standing, ears on stalks, in a ring round Celeste.

'What school do you come from?'

'I don't come from any at all. I've never been to school before.'

'What – *never*?'

'Why *not*?'

Celeste made a little face.

'I wasn't well enough. I had a million headaches, and I was so thin Granny says I could have got lost in a cucumber sandwich. My wobbly knees refused to carry me, and all the doctors said I'd never make old bones.'

She smiled seraphically.

'Then I got better. And so here I am.'

And there she was. But what to do with her? Clearly, she ought to be handed over to one of the teachers. So Penny stood on one side of her and Lisa on the other, and they started to march her, like a prisoner between guards, over the playground and right across Barry Hunter's flight path.

He saw them coming.

Penny's hand tightened round her bag of crisps. Oh, please don't, she thought. Not now. Not with someone new watching.

But already he was screeching round in one of his wide curves.

'Emergency! Emergency! The moving mountain is looming out of the mist! Swerve to avoid a crash! Boy, is she *huge*!'

Celeste stopped walking. She turned to Penny, and asked pleasantly:

'Poor boy. Is he touched with the feather of madness?'

Penny couldn't even try to answer. For one thing she was forcing back hot tears of embarrassment and shame. And for another, she'd never dare say anything about Barry Hunter to someone she didn't know, in case it got back to him and made him worse.

But Lisa wasn't worried.

'That's Barry Hunter,' she was telling Celeste. 'He's a big bully. He bullies everyone.'

Again, Celeste stopped to look back. Now Barry Hunter was tormenting Mark, snatching his pencil-box from him as he steered past.

'Give it back!' Mark said.

'What?'

'That box. It's mine. Give it back.'

The Angel of Nitshill Road

Mark stamped over the playground after Barry. But Barry was quicker on his feet. Prancing and dancing backwards as Mark advanced, he held the box a few inches from Mark's grasping fingers.

'Say please!'

'It's my box. You snatched it. Give it back!'

'Manners! Say please.'

The bell was ringing now.

'Give it back.'

Mr Fairway appeared in the doorway.

'Give it back!'

Mark was almost in tears.

'Say please,' tormented Barry.

'Please,' muttered Mark.

'A bit louder. I can't hear you.'

'*Please*,' shouted Mark in desperation.

'That's not polite,' said Barry. 'Now say it nicely.'

Mark was about to launch himself on his tormentor when suddenly Barry Hunter let out a scream of pain and swirled about, dropping the pencil-box and clutching the back of his leg.

'Who did *that*?' he yelped.

Celeste was standing right behind, eyeing him steadily.

Mr Fairway was very close now.

'What's going on over here?'

Barry knew when to cut his losses. He was about to melt away when Celeste's ringing tones stopped everyone in their tracks.

'I do believe I bit him,' she was telling the teacher.

Mr Fairway was astonished.

'*Bit* him? But *why*?'

Celeste spread her hands and said vaguely:

'Such herds of new faces. One cannot like them *all* . . .'

The bell rang once again. Mr Fairway brushed his hand through his hair.

'Now this isn't a very good start, is it, Celeste?'

Celeste turned her angelic face up towards

him and said cheerfully:

'Oh, scold me if you must. But not so hard I cry, because once I start, I weep buckets.'

Mr Fairway let out a soft moan of horror. He was still standing wondering what to do when the head teacher's voice floated over from the doorway.

'Everyone in line!' Mrs Brown was shouting.

They all obeyed at once, even Barry

Hunter. Lisa took Celeste's hand and led her over to stand next to Penny. Mark fetched up at the very end of the line, as usual, fiddling with his pencil-box and dropping bits and pieces all over the tarmac. But everyone else, even Marigold, stood quietly staring at Celeste.

And no one stared harder than Mr Fairway.

3
'Comfy as a cloud . . .'

Afterwards, no one could remember quite who it was who first guessed she was a real angel. There were enough clues, of course. Tracey overheard Mrs Brown complaining that Celeste had dropped 'out of the blue'. When Ian took the register to the school office he heard the secretary telling Miss Featherstone that the new girl had a 'heavenly' accent. And Mr Fairway was reported to have muttered that Celeste was having 'a bit of trouble coming down to earth'.

Then Lisa remembered that Celeste's father

hadn't walked off that first morning. Or driven. He'd *flown*!

And that reminded Penny. How had Celeste's granny got there in time to stop her being given the wrong name?

She'd *swooped*.

The little group who chummed down Nitshill Road had a chat at the corner.

'So what did Celeste's father want to call her, anyway?'

Penny pushed the sweet she was sucking into the pouch of her cheek, out of the way.

'Angelica, she told us.'

'*Angelica*!'

Another clue!

Tracey raced back just as the bell was ringing for afternoon school. As they pushed and shoved their way back into the classroom, she whispered to everyone round her:

'Guess what Celeste means! I looked it up in our *Name Your Baby* book. Celeste means "from heaven".'

The Angel of Nitshill Road

They all peeped at Celeste. Just at that moment she was gazing up out of her frizzy halo of bright hair, and telling Mr Fairway:

'No, truly, I know this chair's old enough to have a beard, and wobbles frightfully. But it's as comfy as a cloud!'

Comfy as a *cloud*? Penny sneaked a crisp out of the bag on her lap and thought about the one and only time she'd ever gone on holiday by plane. She'd flattened her face against the small plastic window, and seen beneath her a whole land of sunlit fleecy clouds, so puffy and thick you'd think you could bounce on them forever.

So had Celeste –? Did Celeste –?

And she wasn't the only one wondering. The whispers ran round the room.

'Comfy as a cloud!'

'That settles it! How else would anybody *know*?'

'You only have to look at her, really . . .'

Except for Marigold, they were all looking

at her now. There she sat, on her little wobbly chair. Her face glowed as if it were lit from inside with a candle. Her hair shone round her smiling face. She looked like all the angels they had ever seen in books, and films and paintings.

And clearly Mr Fairway thought so too. He didn't treat her just like one of them. Oh, he may have tried his best. But he couldn't do it. It never seemed to work. Somehow it always went wrong, because of her. She wasn't like them. She was different.

Take the day she got up from her desk in the middle of spelling.

Mr Fairway's chalk skidded to a halt on the blackboard.

'Celeste?'

She waved an airy hand.

'Don't let me distract you,' she told him. 'I'm just off to water this poor plant. It's simply *gasping*.'

'Please sit down, Celeste,' Mr Fairway said.

'This is a lesson, and the plant can wait.'

Celeste sat down.

'It's your decision, of course,' she told him kindly. 'But really, without water, that poor plant is not long for this world.'

From that moment on, no one could concentrate on a single word Mr Fairway was saying. They all kept glancing at the poor primula wilting on the windowsill. Even Mr Fairway found that time and again his eyes were drawn back to its parched and drooping leaves.

And in the end he cracked.

'Go on, then,' he told Celeste. 'Water it if you must. But be quick about it.'

She'd done it in a flash.

The next day, when he came in with the register, she was on her feet, busily buffing away at the top of her desk with a soft cloth.

'What's that peculiar smell?' he demanded.

'Marigold,' sniggered Barry Hunter, loudly. Mr Fairway pretended that he hadn't heard, but Celeste looked up anxiously.

'What on earth are you doing, Celeste?' Mr Fairway demanded.

She pushed her hair back from her face and shrugged.

'Heaven knows, I'm not a brilliant housekeeper myself,' she admitted. 'But really, the cleaning in this school is a disgrace! The litter might just as well be a carpet, the way it's all over the floors. And as for the top of this desk, well, I'm afraid that yesterday I could hardly bring myself to rest a tired elbow on it. So I'm polishing it nicely.'

Mr Fairway sat down weakly at his desk. He didn't know what to say. And next morning, when he strolled in the room and found everybody else (except for Marigold) polishing their desks as well, he was quite lost for words.

But not Celeste.

'Ah, there you are!' She beamed at him delightedly. 'We thought you were never

coming! Some of us had quite given up hope.'
Then, while he was still reeling from the smell
of a dozen different polish sprays, she warned
him confidentially: 'Today I'm going to try
and coax you into letting me off arithmetic.
You see, I go all of a tremble with sums. I
always have. I always will. And this morning I
feel weak as a leaf. So mayn't I just loll about
at my desk till I feel a little bit stronger?'

'Now listen here, Celeste –' began Mr
Fairway.

Everyone waited.

But there wasn't any more. Once again, he
was speechless.

Tracey nudged Penny, who was
unwrapping a sweet beneath the desk.

'She *must* be a real angel,' Tracey
explained. 'A normal person couldn't get
away with it. They'd get sent to Mrs Brown.'

Celeste was never sent to Mrs Brown.

She *must* have been a real angel.

4

'Stuck *again*'

Whatever they did in heaven, it wasn't arithmetic. Celeste was awful at maths. Truly awful. She was even worse than Marigold, which was saying something. She was the worst in the class.

By *far*.

Mr Fairway did his best with her.

'Try it again,' he would coax. 'One more time. I'm sure you've nearly got it. You're coming along nicely.'

She'd raise her angelic face to him, her sky-blue eyes round as saucers.

'You can say to me all the pretty things you

want,' she would tell him. 'But I still won't be able to do arithmetic. Who would have thought a few horrid squiggles on a page could make a poor body so unhappy? And there's no hope. Granny says baby girls come either with brains or with yellow hair – never with both.'

'That is the silliest thing I've ever heard!' Mr Fairway cried in a passion.

'There!' Celeste wailed. 'Now you're in a pet with me! Now I shall cry.'

She never did, though. Sometimes she got cross.

'No wonder I can't do it,' she'd scowl at him. 'This classroom is sheer pandemonium. No one could *think*.'

'Tracey and Yusef are managing,' Mr Fairway would point out tartly.

Celeste would sulk.

'And it's so dark in here I can barely see the book!'

Mr Fairway flicked on the light switch.

The Angel of Nitshill Road

'And this pencil must be Mark's. It's chewed down to a *splinter*.'

'Celeste!' Mr Fairway said sternly. 'Stop all this complaining. Just try and get on with it, *please*. I have to go round and help other people.'

She glowered at him from under her blazing hair.

'Very well. Go round and round the class like an old *Beano*! I'll simply sit here and *rust*.'

Relieved, Mr Fairway moved away. He went up and down between the desks, helping people, till he reached Marigold, who was turning over a new page.

'Well done!' he said. 'On page 27 already! At this rate you'll soon be on to the green book!'

Marigold said something. It was so soft he couldn't hear a word. He bent his head closer, and told her:

'Say that again.'

The Angel of Nitshill Road

He didn't expect that she would. But Marigold moved her head very near to his, and whispered in his ear:

'Which page is *she* on?'

He didn't need to be told which *she* Marigold wanted to know about. He simply knew. Normally, he wouldn't answer a question like that (except, of course, to say 'You mind your own business', or 'Don't worry about anyone else. Just get on with your own work'). But Marigold had been the slowest in the class for years and years and years.

He couldn't help it. He just whispered back, 'She's halfway down page 17. And don't tell anybody, but she's stuck *again*.'

Marigold said nothing. But she gripped her pencil and lowered her head determinedly to her work book.

Mr Fairway gave her a little look, then moved forward to the next desk.

Fancy that! he was thinking. Who'd have

believed a little thing like Celeste coming to school here would make such a change in our Marigold? Fancy that!

5
'Fat! Fat! Fat! Fat!'

And it wasn't the only change, either. From the moment Celeste first appeared in the gateway, all sorts of things started to happen. You take the day that Barry Hunter circled Penny with his usual cry of 'Moving mountain!' and fetched up on the tarmac like a winded ten-ton starfish.

Celeste had stuck out a foot and tripped him up.

He rolled over, blood on his hands and knees. Celeste didn't wait for him to attack. She attacked first.

'My granny says you must have been born in a bucket!' she told him. 'You have no manners and you have no brains. Now stop calling Penny fat!'

Barry Hunter thought he'd got her there.

'I didn't say "fat". *You* did.'

Celeste gave him one of her scornful looks.

'Moving mountain means *fat*,' she told him. 'Fat! Fat! Fat! Fat! But what you don't seem to realise is that if Penny stopped stuffing her face with crisps and sweeties all day long, she'd soon be as thin as I am. But you!' She pointed to him as if he were a slug on the ground. 'You're a bully! And it's harder to change that. If you're not careful, no one will ever really like you!'

Now he was scrambling to his feet, fit to kill.

'You'll be sorry!' he snarled. 'You wait!'

But Celeste had already turned away. The only thing he could have done was throw himself on her for a real fight. But she was dressed, as usual, in pure and perfect white. And she was smaller than he was. And her back was turned.

And everyone except Marigold was watching . . .

'I'll get you next break!' he yelled at her. 'You wait and see!'

'When donkeys fly!' Celeste cat-called back, and strode off with Penny. Penny was crying hard. She couldn't help it. No one had ever called her fat before. Not yelled it out like that, for everyone to hear. Oh, she knew they sometimes whispered the horrible word behind her back, out of her hearing. Even her friends did that, since it was true.

But for Celeste to shout it out like that, all over the playground!

The tears rolled down Penny's cheeks. Fat! Fat! Fat! Fat! She heard it ringing in her ears like a bell. Fat! Fat! Fat! Fat! So she couldn't understand why it was Celeste's arm she had around her shoulders. And why the grippy feeling deep inside had loosened up a bit. Was it because she knew that, next break, Barry Hunter wouldn't be bothering to run round the playground being spiteful to her? Was that it? Because she knew that, for the first time as long as she could remember, she'd probably be safe.

Barry would be after Celeste.

He tried his old trick – the one he usually played on Mark: blocking the lavatories. He'd never played it on a girl before, but they knew

what was going on the moment they saw him and his gang lined up across the entrance to the *Girls*.

Sean, Wayne, Barry himself and Stephen, who was sent round the back to block the tiny window: the whole gang.

When other girls tried to go in, the boys let them pass. Even Marigold went in without any trouble except for the usual sniffing and cries of 'What's that awful smell?' But when Celeste tried to walk past, the boys moved in quickly to push her back.

Celeste tried walking in with Lisa and Penny. All three of them were pushed back.

Lisa tried going in alone. This time, Barry Hunter and his gang didn't stop her. At the top of the steps, Lisa turned and looked back doubtfully.

'You might as well go in,' Celeste called out cheerfully. 'It's only sensible.'

So Lisa went in.

When she came out, Celeste tried again,

and she was pushed back, hard.

Then Penny tried. Again, the gang stood aside to let Penny pass. Penny, too, looked back towards Celeste, not knowing what to do.

'Go ahead,' Celeste called out. 'Before the bell rings and it's too late for you.'

So Penny went in as well.

When she appeared again, Celeste tried one last time. Sean and Wayne pushed her back, while Barry Hunter stood with his arms folded, smirking.

Shrugging, Celeste strolled away.

Barry Hunter and his gang stayed where they were, ready to block the lavatories against Celeste, right through the break. They kept an eye on her each time she ambled past, arm in arm with Lisa and Penny. She came just close enough each time to keep them on their guard. But she didn't seem bothered. And she certainly wasn't desperate. In fact, she seemed to be the most unruffled person in the playground, because everyone else was rushing from one knot of friends to the next, chattering excitedly.

Just before the bell rang, some of the other girls came near Barry Hunter's gang outside the lavatories. They giggled and pointed and stuffed their hands over their mouths. But Barry didn't realise they were laughing at him until Mr Fairway called him sharply into line, and he heard the whispers for the very first time.

'Haven't you *heard*?'

'Celeste went into the *Boys*!'

'She just walked straight in there!'

'Into the *Boys*!'

And Mr Fairway heard, too. He stared down at Celeste who was, as usual, gazing up at him with her imperturbable smile. Surely it couldn't be true! Not even Celeste . . . !

No! It must be one of those silly tales that runs round and round a school.

He took another worried peep at her.
No! Surely not even Celeste!

6
'Normal'

While Mr Fairway was fetching the register from the office, Barry Hunter took his bad temper out on Mark.

'Shake!' he said, stopping him getting to his desk, and shoving his hand out.

Mark put his own hands safely behind his back and shook his head.

'Leave me alone,' he muttered. 'I wasn't bothering you.'

'That isn't very nice,' said Barry. 'I only want to make friends properly.'

He grinned in his lordly way at everyone

who was sitting there, silently watching.

'Go on,' he told Mark again. 'Shake hands.'

Mark tried to back away between the desks. But Barry Hunter followed him.

'Shake, and I'll give you a sweetie,' he wheedled, as if he were talking to a baby. When she heard the word 'sweetie', Penny's hand slid automatically into her pocket. Then she remembered that as she was walking into Mr Hamid's shop that morning, she'd suddenly heard Celeste's pure clear voice ringing like an echo in her brain: 'If Penny stopped stuffing her face with crisps and sweeties all day long, she'd soon be as thin as I am!' Something had made her just wave at Mr Hamid, then turn and walk out. So now she sat quietly clinking the coins that were still in her pocket, while she watched Mark going red in the face, and saying:

'I don't want a sweetie.'

He turned away. But Barry Hunter was too quick for him. Catching Mark by the arm, he forced him round and squeezed his hand so tightly that Mark yelped.

Then he gave Mark's wrist a twist-burn.

'See!' he crowed. 'I told you I'd give you a sweetie! A big barley sugar!'

The tears rolled down behind Mark's spectacles. He stumbled off blindly, just as Mr Fairway came back through the door.

'Stop clattering about, Mark!' said Mr Fairway. 'Sit *down*.'

The Angel of Nitshill Road

All afternoon Barry Hunter made life difficult for poor old Mark. He tripped him up when he was called to Mr Fairway's desk. While Mark was up there, Barry took Mark's pencil-box and hid it behind the books in the corner. He dropped Mark's woolly on the floor and trod a huge footprint on it. And when Mr Fairway went out to fetch some more paper, Barry stood on his chair and announced that Mark gave walking-funny lessons every Saturday morning down at Marigold's smelly old church.

Marigold just sat there pretending she wasn't listening. But Mark took the chance of Mr Fairway being out of the room to crash about, trying to find his pencil-box.

'Sit *down*!' Mr Fairway said when he came back. 'I'm sick of telling you, Mark! Stay at your desk!'

'But –'

'No *buts*. Just sit there, *please*, and stop disturbing everyone.'

Celeste rose to her feet.

'I think you ought to know –' she began to explain.

But Mr Fairway had had enough.

'Sit down, Celeste,' he said. 'When I want your opinion, I'll ask for it.'

Celeste sat down. All afternoon she never spoke a word. Mr Fairway smiled at her several times, trying to cajole her into answering questions he knew perfectly well she could get right. Each time she coldly turned her face away and gazed pointedly out of the window. Every few minutes she glanced at her watch, and drummed her fingers lightly on the desk top.

Mr Fairway was as glad as the rest of them when the last bell rang.

Out in the corridor, Barry Hunter pushed his way over to Celeste. You could tell from the look on his face that he was going to pay her out for trying to tell on him.

Calmly, Celeste waited till he was two feet

away, then opened her mouth and screamed. Everyone stopped shoving towards the two cloakrooms and turned to stare. No one had ever heard anything like it. You'd think a police car had switched on its siren inside a biscuit tin. The noise was prodigious.

Barry Hunter backed off, fast.

As promptly as she'd turned the scream on, Celeste turned it off again.

'You'll catch it if Mrs Brown heard that,' Barry Hunter jeered.

'You'll catch it, too,' warned Celeste. 'I'll tell her all the things you did to Mark.'

Just as she said his name, Mark stumbled out of the classroom, last as usual, and tripped over one of his own feet.

Barry Hunter snorted with amusement.

'I don't know why you keep sticking up for him,' he said scornfully to Celeste. 'He's *weird*.'

Mark's face went scarlet.

'I'm not weird!'

The Angel of Nitshill Road

'Well, you're not *normal*, are you?' taunted Barry. He poked Mark in the chest, and peered closely at his face through the thick bottle glasses, as if he were looking at some insect through a microscope. 'No. You couldn't say you were *normal*.'

Suddenly Celeste was there, between the two of them.

'And you *are*, are you?' she demanded.

She turned to everyone in the corridor – not just the people from their own class, but everyone else who was shuffling into the cloakrooms.

'Who wants to be *normal*, if normal's like Barry Hunter? Barry Hunter's a bully! He's spiteful and horrid! He steals and hides things! He's a slyboots and his only real pleasure comes from making the people round him unhappy! So who wants to be *normal*?'

She gazed round.

'Come on! Speak up! Say if you want to be *normal*!'

The dead silence in the corridor spread to the cloakrooms on either side. Everyone was watching Barry Hunter and Celeste. But no one said a word.

'Right!' Celeste yelled, turning back to him. 'Now you know, don't you! No one in this whole school wants to be normal, if being normal means being like *you*!'

Dumbstruck, the whole school watched as she slammed out.

Barry Hunter shrugged.

'She's mad,' he announced. 'She's completely off her rocker. I reckon she's even more weird than Mark the Martian. She ought to be locked up.'

One or two of them caught his eye, but nobody grinned or nodded. Nobody answered him. He was on his own. Too many of them were thinking privately how nice it would be if Barry Hunter was locked up. Or locked out. Or run over. Or *dead*. Over the years, he'd ruined so many lessons, spoiled so many games, made so many of them so unhappy. Hardly a child in the school could not remember lying in bed, dreading the day to come, thinking how wonderful school could be if people like Barry Hunter were kept in control, and they could get on with their work and enjoy their breaks – just have a normal day.

A normal school day. Wouldn't that be *weird?*

7
Round Robin

Next morning, Celeste came into school holding a big black book. Its cover was patterned with gold. Tucked down its spine was a gold pen that wrote in eight separate colours. You could choose which you wanted by twisting a fat knob.

'What's in the book, Celeste?'

'These pages are all *blank*.'

'Are you going to write in it?'

All she would tell them was:

'Wait and see.'

They didn't have to wait long. Only a few

minutes later Barry Hunter came swooping round the corner, saw Marigold, and stopped to sniff.

'What's that foul smell? Is it you, Marigold?'

Marigold turned away.

He followed, sniffing ostentatiously. Then he swooped off again. When Marigold turned back, Celeste was behind her, holding the black book.

'Now what *exactly* did he say to you?'

Marigold smeared the tears across her cheek, and tried to pretend she hadn't heard.

'Come on,' Celeste ordered. 'Unbutton your beak! I have to write it down.'

Marigold stared. She stared at Celeste, then at the black book in her hand. Her eyes widened in amazement.

Then, though her eyes filled with tears when she had to repeat it, she answered Celeste's question.

'He said, "What's that foul smell? Is it you, Marigold?"'

Celeste wrote it down. Everyone crowded round to watch as Celeste's golden pen moved steadily across the lines of the black book, writing the date and time neatly in the margin, then everything that happened, down to the fact that Marigold was crying.

'You needn't put that in,' Lisa said.

Celeste ignored her. Very carefully, right at the end, she twisted the knob round from black to blue, and printed neatly:

The Angel of Nitshill Road

WITNESSES:

Then she looked up.

'Who wants to be first witness?'

Nobody wanted to be first witness.

'We'll just have to do a round robin, then,' she informed them.

'What's a round robin?'

She showed them.

'Put your name here,' she ordered Mark, pointing to the bottom of the page.

Where she was pointing seemed very far away from anything she'd written. And he was dying to have a go with the fancy gold pen.

'Can I choose the colour, and twist the knob myself?'

'Yes.'

Mark couldn't resist. He had to fiddle the knob round four times before he managed to stop on the right colour. But then, triumphantly, he scratched his name in glorious fern green.

She took the pen out of his hand, and gave it to Lisa.

'And you sign your name here.'

The spot she chose was right on the edge, miles away from the writing. And Lisa longed to write her name in silver.

'Penny.'

Way over the other side, where Celeste was pointing, Penny chose to write her name in gold. As she was doing it, she wondered how much the pen had cost. She'd saved quite a bit of money already, not buying any more crisps or sweets.

'Paul.'

He didn't hesitate.

'I'm first to use the red!'

Everyone was queuing now, keen to have a go at twisting the knob of the fancy gold pen to choose the colour for their name.

'Tracey.'

'Yusef.'

The Angel of Nitshill Road

'Kelly.'

She called out names till there was hardly anybody left. Then:

'Marigold.'

Marigold shook her head.

'Go on,' everyone urged her.

She shook her head again.

'Why not?'

'We've all written our names.'

'Come on, Marigold.'

'Are you scared?'

She didn't look scared. But then again, as usual she didn't really look anything. And she didn't say anything, either. She simply stared down at the ground at her feet, and shook her head again.

Celeste turned to look for someone else.

'Wayne.'

'*Me*?'

He was only hanging about on the edge out of sheer nosiness. Usually he was part of Barry Hunter's gang. But that didn't seem to bother Celeste.

'Did you hear what he said, or didn't you?'

'Well, yes –'

'Then sign.'

Wayne hesitated. He didn't know what she was going to do with what she'd written and everyone had signed. And Barry Hunter would kill him. But, on the other hand, he really wanted to write his name in the purple.

And one more name couldn't matter.

'Where shall I put it?'

Celeste handed him the book. It was quite obvious where he should write his name. Once his was done, under Celeste's report would be a perfect ring of brightly-coloured names – no first, no last; just a circle of witnesses with no leader, no head of the gang.

Wayne signed.

'There,' said Celeste. 'That's a round robin.'

They all stared at it gravely. Then the bell rang. While they were trooping into class, Penny asked Marigold:

The Angel of Nitshill Road

'Why wouldn't you write in Celeste's book?'

She never expected Marigold to answer. More often than not, if you asked Marigold a question, she just pretended that she hadn't heard.

Not this time, though. For the first time ever, Marigold looked Penny straight in the eye.

'It's wrong,' she said. 'You shouldn't have written your name, either. Nobody should. Only the angel can write in the Book of Deeds.'

Marigold walked off, leaving Penny gaping.

Book of Deeds? What on earth?

She glanced uneasily towards Celeste.

Of course, with an angel, the question might not be 'What on earth?' at all.

It might be 'What in heaven?'

8
The Book of Deeds

Everyone sat in a circle round Marigold.

'Tell us again,' Kelly told her.

Marigold wriggled on the step.

'I've *told* you,' she said. 'I've told you everything I know a dozen times.'

'Tell us again.'

Marigold took a deep breath and told them again. Each time she told the story she added on a little bit she'd never said before. This was partly because the story seemed to grow inside her each time they made her tell it, and partly because she wanted to keep them interested. It was quite nice to sit up on the step with everyone gathered round, listening hard. It kept her safe from Barry Hunter. And it was a bit like having lots of friends.

She told them all over again.

'I heard about it in church. There is an angel who is beautiful and perfect and stands at heaven's gate –'

'Like she stood at ours.'

All eyes swivelled to the gates through which, at any moment, they expected her.

'And this angel has a name, the Recording Angel, because his job –'

'*Her* job –'

'The angel's job is to write everything you ever did in your whole life – whether it's good or bad – down neatly in the Book of Deeds.'

Last time she'd added 'neatly'. This time she embroidered the story a little bit more.

'If it was a good deed, the angel smiles writing it down.'

'She smiles a lot.'

The Angel of Nitshill Road

'And if it's a bad deed, the angel weeps.'

There was a slightly embarrassed pause. No one liked to mention that Celeste never wept. Oh, they couldn't count the number of times she'd said to Mr Fairway: 'Don't make me finish my sums. It isn't worth it. I'll just sit and *howl*.' But, so far, no one had ever seen a single tear in her eye.

Marigold knew what they were thinking, but she pressed on anyway.

'But even the angel's tears can't wash out what is written down. Whatever the deed was, it stays in the book for ever and ever.'

There was the usual grave silence. Ian held out his crisp bag and everyone except Penny dipped in to take one while they had a think. Then Kelly said:

'He's going to be in such trouble when he gets to heaven's gate. She's used up half the book already, writing down the horrid things he does.'

'She never makes anything up, though.' Yusef defended Celeste.

'The truth, the whole truth, and nothing but the truth,' said Elaine.

Their eyes searched out Barry Hunter. He was over the other side of the playground, all alone, kicking a box to bits. Over the last weeks, his gang had dwindled to almost no one. Wayne never even tried to make friends again, after being a witness in Celeste's book. He just went off with Stephen, who was pretty fed up with always being the one sent round the back to guard the window when they blocked the lavatories. That only left Sean. And Sean was often off school.

So Barry Hunter spent more and more of his time mucking about by himself. He was still bullying, but it wasn't the same now that each time he tried it a dozen people came running from far and wide to watch him do his worst, all shouting eagerly:

'Bags be first witness!'

The Angel of Nitshill Road

'No! Let *me*!'

There was still plenty for the Book of Deeds, though. When Celeste opened it on any page, everyone would peer over her shoulder to read it.

Thursday, 4 May

8.46 Barry Hunter wouldn't stop putting his head under Mark's toilet door when he needed to be private. He said it was 'only a joke'.

Witnesses: Ian. Wayne. Yusef. Mark.

8.56 Barry Hunter kept bumping into people on the way to Assembly. He said 'Stop bumping' loudly to everyone he bumped, but it was really him bumping. Paul, Nessa and Zabeen say he wasn't bumping hard, he was just annoying. Wayne says his bump really hurt (and he had to bump back a bit).

Witnesses: Wayne. Zabeen. Nessa. Celeste. Kelly. Ian. Lisa. Penny. Phil.

Paul. Mark. Elaine. Yusef. (And Mr Fairway gave Barry one of his looks, so he must have seen too.)

9.50   Barry Hunter sniffed near Marigold and said, 'What's that horrible smell?' twice.

9.51   He did it again.

9.53   And again.

Witnesses: Lisa. Penny. Ian. Phil. Nessa. (We didn't ask Marigold because she was upset, and she doesn't sign anyway.)

10.30   Barry Hunter ruined Claire and Elaine's Fashion Show. First he hid some of the clothes behind the pipes, so there wasn't much time left. Then, when the people in the show were taking their turns to show their fashions off, he started booing loudly. So everyone in the show got embarrassed and wouldn't do it properly. So Mr Fairway stopped the show. (Barry Hunter wasn't the *only* one to boo, but he was *definitely* the one who started it.)

Witnesses: Claire. Elaine. Phil. Ian. Zabeen. Tracey. P.T.O.

And all that was just on one page. No wonder everyone crowded round Marigold, keen to hear any tiny thing she could remember about what happened with a Book of Deeds. No wonder, when Celeste finally sailed through the gates, her gleaming frock mirroring the shine of her hair, her eyes bright with excitement, everyone (even Marigold) ran over to greet her.

'Where have you *been*?'

Celeste spread her hands.

'Disaster! Last night I cried so much I had to peg up my pillowcase. I'm being moved.'

'Moved?'

Everyone was horrified.

'Moved *where*?'

'Moved *how*?'

'*Why*?'

Celeste settled on the step, and tucked her frock neatly around her.

'Blame my father entirely!' she told them. 'Granny has told him time and again that trying to teach me arithmetic is like trying to plough the sea. But he won't rest. First he harped on about it, day and night. Now it seems he's been flitting from school to school, green with worry, looking for somewhere a dilly like me can learn to slap eight and eight together, and make fourteen.'

'Sixteen,' they corrected her, but she wasn't listening. She was far too excited.

'And so I'm to be swept off again, like a loose leaf tumbling around the world.'

'But where?'

'When?'

She made a face.

'Almost at once. Would you believe, I've even had to beg for these few hours to totter in and exchange a few sad farewells!'

In the shocked silence that followed, the ringing of the bell came almost as a relief.

Celeste rose to her feet, sighing, and brushed an invisible speck from her frock.

'Come along,' she told them. 'Let's go and break the news. I shall sob so hard Mr Fairway will have to mop all the floors behind me as I go.'

Appalled, they set off in a bunch across the playground. Her eyes still shining, she strolled after them.

9
'Only a joke.
Only a game.'

Before they reached the school door, they heard Barry Hunter shouting.

'Bombs away!'

Everyone spun round to watch as Barry swung back his foot and, giving the old box one last tremendous boot, sent it flying – up, up, up and over.

It landed – plop! – on top of poor Mark's head.

'Bull's eye!' yelled Barry Hunter.

They all stood waiting for Mark to tear the box off his head. They were waiting for the red face. They were waiting for the tears and the temper. Tracey said, 'Bags be first witness,' and everyone else looked round to check that Celeste was carrying her big black book and her fancy gold pen.

Mark staggered round the playground like a robot out of control.

Above Penny's head, the staff-room window opened, and she heard Mrs Brown ask Mr

Fairway anxiously:

'Is he *hurt*?'

Like everyone in the playground, Mr Fairway watched Mark swivel his head round as if he were looking for radio signals.

'No,' Penny heard him say. 'I think he's actually making a bit of a joke of it.'

Mrs Brown sounded astonished.

'Mark? Making a joke of something Barry Hunter did to him? Now there's a change!'

Just at that moment, Marigold ran up to offer Mark a guiding hand.

'Am I *dreaming*?' said Mrs Brown. 'Is that *Marigold* who just ran up and joined in the game?'

'She was telling them all Bible stories yesterday,' said Miss Featherstone.

'I don't believe it!' Mrs Brown said. Then, glancing down, she noticed Penny just beneath the window. Quickly, Penny ran off, pretending she was going to help Marigold steer Mark away from all the people standing

round clapping his brilliant robot act. The last thing she overheard was Mrs Brown saying:

'Really, that child Penny's clothes are practically falling off her! It's time she tightened her buttons.'

For the twentieth time that day, Penny hitched her skirt up and grinned. She wasn't going to tighten her buttons. Not yet! Having your clothes flapping was much nicer than having them bulging.

Now Marigold had lifted the battered old box off Mark's head. The joke was over, so Penny joined the gang of people crowding round Celeste.

'Can I be first and sign in the silver?'

'Let me be yellow!'

'Bags be green!'

But Celeste hadn't even opened the black book.

'There's nothing to write,' she told them. 'Everyone had a good time. If someone's unhappy, then it goes in the book. If everyone's happy, then it doesn't.'

They all thought about it for a moment. It seemed fair enough, as rules went. Much fairer, anyway, than letting Barry Hunter get away with making people miserable and then saying: 'Only a joke. Only a game.'

Yes. It was a good way to judge.

Content, they watched Celeste tuck the black book safely away under her arm. Content, they followed her into the school.

10
Goodbye, Celeste

'The bell hasn't rung yet,' said Mrs Brown. 'Why is everyone in your class except Barry Hunter inside?'

Mr Fairway sighed and put his mug down on the draining board.

'Blame Celeste,' he said. 'Since she came, none of them have been the same.'

Mrs Brown glanced at him thoughtfully.

'Perhaps that's no bad thing,' she said. 'When you remember how some of them were before.'

He thought about that all down the

corridor. It was so much on his mind that when the school secretary popped her head round the office door and said, 'Guess who's leaving?' he answered right first time.

'Celeste!'

So *that* was why the whole lot had trooped in before the bell. To bring him the sad news. And he *was* sad. She was a strange little creature, but he would miss her.

He pushed the classroom door open.

There they all stood in a half circle around her. Celeste had even more of a glow than usual on her face. In fact, she looked radiant.

'Well!' he said, sitting heavily at his desk. 'This is a sad day!'

She gave him one of her celestial smiles.

'I have something for you,' she told him, and nodded to Marigold, who stepped up and gave him a black book patterned with gold. At first, from the solemn way she handed it over, he thought that it must be a Bible. But then he realised it was the book he'd seen them poring over so often in the playground. And in the cloakrooms. And in class.

'Thank you,' he said, and opened it to take a look inside.

It was a shock. A horrid, horrid book. An ugly catalogue of pain and humiliation and fear and spite. He felt sick reading it. He turned over two or three more pages, feeling all their eyes on him, then raised his own to Celeste.

'Is this really what you're leaving me?' he asked. 'A book of tale-telling.'

Celeste said steadily:

'Granny says the rule not to tell tales was invented by bullies –' Her sky-blue eyes met his across the desk. 'And the people who don't really want to stand up to them.'

He couldn't meet her gaze any longer. He looked down. Another horrid passage caught his eye. He read it to the end. Oh, poor, poor Marigold! No wonder she went round pretending to be deaf, if that's what she heard

all day! And Mark! The number of times he must have been tricked into getting into trouble. And Penny! 'Moving mountain' indeed! And all the other things that happened to the rest. How horrible to be kept from using the lavatory, or fetching your coat! How nasty to have your things snatched and hidden all day long! Your games ruined, your family called rude names, your jacket torn and muddied.

'Why didn't anyone tell me all this was going on?'

Those sky-blue eyes again. She didn't answer. She knew as well as he did, as well as they all did, that he'd known everything he needed all along. But just like Marigold he had pretended not to see, not to hear, not to understand.

He slammed the book shut so hard it made them jump.

'Right!' he said. 'I've read enough!'

This time he managed to meet her eye. He really meant what he said.

'Things will be very different around here from now on.'

'You promise to keep the book?'

'Here in my desk,' he promised her. 'As long as I'm teaching in this school.'

'Just to remind you . . .'

'To remind me.'

Again, their eyes met. She was satisfied. Smiling, she stuck out her hand.

'Well, then. Goodbye,' she said, as if she were leaving a party. 'Thank you very much for having me. I hope I haven't been too much trouble.'

Mr Fairway came round the desk. Blinking his tears away, he gave her a giant hug.

'Trouble?' he said. 'Nonsense! Listen, Celeste. Wherever you go, I want you to tell them that we thought you were a real *angel*. And in the few weeks we were lucky enough to have you at Nitshill Road School, you have worked *wonders*.'

She hugged him back. Then she hugged everyone else. Then she was off. On her way to the door, she dropped the gold pen on to Barry Hunter's desk, and turned to wink at them.

And even those who were astonished winked back.

BiLL'S NEW FROCK

Bill Simpson wakes up to find he's a girl, and, worse, his mother makes him wear a frilly pink dress to school. How on earth is he going to survive a whole day like this?

Everything just seems to be *different* for girls . . .

'Stylishly written and thought-provoking' *Guardian*

'. . . a gem. Don't miss it.' *TES*

WINNER OF THE SMARTIES PRIZE

How To WRite rEallY BAdLY

Chester Howard can see Joe's project 'How to Write Neatly' can only be a disaster. Bottom of the class, Joe makes a terrible mess of his work, jumbling letters and numbers up together.

But a project called 'How to Write Really Badly' – now there's something Joe can do better than anyone else.

And Chester is about to find there's a lot more to Joe than he expected . . .

'Screamingly funny' *The Herald*

'Fine has a rare genius for building a funny, enriching and moving story around the nuts and bolts of school life'
The Times

WINNER OF THE *TES* NASEN AWARD

'The chicken gave it to me'

Gemma doesn't believe a chicken could have written a book – chickens can't even read! But here in front of them is *The True Story of Harrowing Farm*, and its scratchy pages definitely look, well, *chickeny*.

It is an epic tale of cruelty and bravery, the story of a chicken who flies frillions of miles, reaching the heights of intergalactic superstardom, to try to save us humans . . .

'a clever and biting social fable . . . wit and brilliance sparkle on every page.' *Junior Bookshelf*

'a terrific little book . . .' Joanna Lumley

Press Play

Mum's not there to get Nicky, Tasha and Little Joe up and out to school that morning. But she's left a mysterious note on top of the cassette player. It just says 'Press Play'.

The three children follow Mum's simple instructions. Well, they try to anyway – with hilarious results.

'very successful . . . there are plenty of laughs'
Times Educational Supplement

The Country Pancake

Lancelot's lovely teacher, Miss Mirabelle, is in big trouble.

She's told a giant whopper and unless she can come up with a brilliant plan, she's going to look very, *very* silly.

Can Lancelot help this damsel in distress?

'this entirely charming tale of an unconventional teacher, a suspicious head, an imaginative class and a co-operative cow.' *TES*